# Akeem

## Tracee Newman

To my incredible family who I love more than life,
you are my hope and my inspiration.

# Table of Contents

# CHAPTER 1

—⚏—

O ne hot summer day, Akeem sat idly by as his grandfather Shakem worked on a bamboo chair. The chair
had some broken reeds in the seat. Shakem worked hard.
He was not a rich man, so he had to make the things he
owned last.

Shakem's house was a small wood frame house with
openings for windows and doors. Across the top of the
door was nailed a long piece of canvas, which hung
straight to the floor. To allow the breeze to blow through,
Shakem would pull the cloth to the side and tie it. The
windows also had canvas coverings that were kept pulled
back except for when it rained.

There were two rooms - the kitchen, and the front room
where Shakem lived and slept. In the kitchen was a por-
celain sink with a hand pump to bring in water. He had a
wood-burning stove and an icebox which would keep food
cool if ice was purchased and put in the top. On the back of
his house was a wooden overhang under which he worked
and kept his tools. Behind the house, the dirt had been
plowed. Vegetables and fruit trees were growing under the
hot sun.

Sometimes Akeem would bring things from his mother which needed to be fixed. Akeem liked coming to his grandfather's house because while his grandfather worked, he told Akeem many stories, as grandfathers often do. On this particular day, Shakem was telling again the story of the white missionary who had come and brought them food and clothes. Akeem had heard this story many times but never tired of the look on his grandfather's face and the joy he shared in telling it...

"It was many years ago... our people were unsettled. We lived in huts and hunted the wild animals for food. Our clothing was simple. The men wore loincloths and the women wore a sort of animal skin skirt. Many had bones or animal teeth pierced through their ears and noses. The women would take care of the children and teach them to make crude weapons or tools and how to build fires.

"They would also teach them of the great many superstitions and myths that our people believed in. We would have ceremonies in the evening with big bonfires and sacrifice animals. Then the seer of the tribe would consult the stars for wisdom and guidance. We would call upon the leaders of the tribe who had died and ask them to come and speak to us from beyond the grave.

"Then one day, a missionary came to our camp and brought us clothes. He brought shoes for our children's feet and shirts for our women. He brought us food from a far-off land, rice and beans, and he showed our women how to cook them with water from the nearby river.

"The missionary became our friend. He stayed many months with our tribe living in a hut that we built for him. At night, he would always sing this same song. The words said:

> *Oh! How I Love Jesus,*
> *Oh, how I love Jesus,*
> *Oh, how I love Jesus*
> *Because He first loved me.*

"As he would sing, tears would well up in his eyes and then one by one slowly trickle down his cheeks. Every night he would sing, and every night he would cry for this Jesus.

"One night, after we had finished our meal, he went into his hut to sing. Several of the men including me followed him. We asked him what this song was that he always sang – this, 'Oh! How I love Jesus!' And we asked him, 'What does it mean?'

"He asked us to sit down with him, and he started to tell us about this friend of his. As he spoke of Him, his eyes would shine and his words would become somber and authoritative. Jesus was very special to him. Perhaps He would also come and visit our tribe, we thought. The missionary told us of how Jesus would come, but only if we invited Him.

"We wanted our newfound missionary friend to be happy, so we said we would invite this Jesus for him. Our friend said He would not come because we wanted Him to come for our missionary, but only if we wanted Him to come for ourselves. This we did not understand. Why would Jesus not come to see

His friend? The missionary taught us the words to his song, and we sang with him before we went to our own huts to sleep.

"Many nights passed. Every night, we would go to hear this missionary talk of his friend. How excited he would be as he told of the many miracles this Jesus would do. We thought Jesus must be a great medicine man and have many voodoo powers. The missionary would tell us that Jesus is greater than all the voodoo powers in the earth. He would also tell of how Jesus would counsel him and tell him where to go and what to do.

"We said, 'Oh, He is like our forefathers who have gone to be one of the stars whom we consult and ask for guidance.'

"The missionary said, 'No, Jesus is greater than the stars for He had created the stars and hung them into place.' I thought, 'How can this be? One so great that He created the heavens themselves?'

"The missionary's face beamed and radiated such a warm and loving glow as he spoke of Jesus that soon, we all wanted to meet Him. We gathered together in a tribal meeting and decided to invite Him to come to our tribe. It was not because we wanted Him to come for our missionary friend, but because we wanted to know Him for ourselves.

"The next morning we gathered with the missionary friend and told him of our decision. The missionary was pleased, but said that there was something very important about Jesus that he had not yet told us.

"'What could this be?' we wondered. 'Maybe He would not want to come so far as the missionary had to come.' We so wanted to know Him, and now we were afraid he would not come.

"The missionary told us of how Jesus had come a long time ago to free the world from sin and that He would come to us, but not as a man comes. He would come and live in our hearts and forgive us for the bad things we had done. The missionary called these things sin.

"I knew right away that I wanted Jesus to come and live in my heart. We prayed a simple prayer, and such peace and contentment flooded me that I will never forget it. Many prayed the prayer that day.

"The missionary stayed for two more years after that and taught us much about Jesus' life and the way that is right to live. No more did we make sacrifices to other gods. We very much wanted to please God."

"Akeem! Akeem," his mother called from outside the house, interrupting the story, "time to come home now!"

Akeem looked at his grandfather. There was no need to say goodbye for they both knew that he would be back tomorrow as soon as his schoolwork was done. Akeem stood up and headed for the door while his grandfather put down the chair he was working on, picked up his tools and went to start his dinner.

Dumaka, Akeem's father, worked at the local diamond mine. His mother stayed home and took care of Akeem and the home. His parents had been married for eleven years and had just recently been able to buy a little, wood frame house with two bedrooms and running water.

Kamaria, Akeem's mother, sat on the couch mending a tear in a shirt with a needle and thread. Dumaka stood in the kitchen washing his hands and face from his day's work. He came home covered in dust and dirt. He looked in at Kamaria as he told her of the day's events.

Dumaka was a happy man. He was always cheerful, and he had a light countenance. He was a man whom people loved to be around because something about him would cheer them up. Akeem stood in the kitchen next to his dad and listened to him. There had been good news that day at work. One of his friends at the mine had many sorrows. Dumaka had been talking to him for several weeks, and the friend had been feeling greatly encouraged.

Dumaka finished washing his hands and dried them on the towel. Then he grabbed Akeem around the waist and lifted him slightly off the ground as he tickled his ribs. Akeem giggled and screamed wildly as he wriggled to get away. He broke loose and ran into the other room. His dad chased him and scooped him up as he sat hard on the couch next to Kamaria.

"Akeem, you are getting so big," his father said. "We better get some food into you." He looked at Kamaria, "Is supper ready?"

She nodded *yes*, put down her mending, and went to set the table. The dinner conversation was especially light and jovial that night. They always had a good time when they were together as a family, but tonight was just different.

After dinner, Akeem went to his room to work on his homework. He could hear his parents talking and laughing as they washed the dishes. He finished his homework and got ready for bed. When he was just about ready his father came in, "Are you ready for bed?"

Akeem answered, "Just about," as he drew the string on his loose cotton pajama bottoms. He hopped in his bed and lay down. His dad sat on the edge while Akeem said his prayers. "Dear God, please bless Mom and Dad and Grandpa. Forgive me of my sins. Help me to do well at school. Amen."

Then his dad kissed him and tucked him in. On his way out, he shut off the light and closed the door.

# CHAPTER 2

A s Akeem walked to his grandfather's house the following afternoon, he passed a small bush and heard hissing inside. Cautiously, he turned in the direction of the sound. The bush hissed again. Akeem's heart raced. "What should I do?" thought Akeem.

Although Akeem lived in a village, there were still wild animals living in the surrounding desert and many were dangerous. Hissssss!

Akeem jumped! He was just about to turn and run when he heard a faint meow. Akeem moved in slowly, pushing back the brush with his foot. There, under the dried, sagebrush-like bristles was a small leopard cub. Akeem picked up the cub. The cub hissed and spit.

"Don't be afraid, little guy," said Akeem, "I'm not going to hurt you. Where is your mother?" Akeem stroked the frightened cub behind the ears. The cub licked Akeem's hand. "You sure are a tiny one. You can't be more than a couple of weeks old. How did you get here?"

The cub cried soft, tiny mews. His voice was hoarse. Akeem knew the leopard cub was much too little to be left alone in the wild. "I guess I'm going to have to take you with me, little one."

The cub meowed as if answering him.

"What shall I call you, brave one? Let's see," thought Akeem. "How about Trakee? That is the name of a brave warrior my grandfather once told me about."

The cub meowed again.

Akeem laughed, "Well, that's it then, my friend. I shall call you Trakee. You must be starving, I must get you to grandfather's. He will know how to feed a baby leopard."

Akeem tucked the cub into his shirt where it was dark and warm. This made Trakee feel safe and, wearied from his frightening ordeal, he soon fell asleep.

As Akeem neared his grandfather's house, he saw Shakem outside cutting some turnips for his dinner. "Grandfather!" he yelled, "Wait till you see." Akeem cupped his hands around Trakee and ran the rest of the way.

"Grandfather, grandfather, look what I have found." Akeem unbuttoned his shirt and pulled the cub out.

Shakem liked animals. "Well, what have we here, my son, a baby leopard? His mother must have run into danger to have gone off and left one so small. We will have to make some meal for him, or he will not last long. What will you call your newfound friend?"

"I'm naming him Trakee, Grandfather," said Akeem.

"Ah, the brave warrior." Shakem took Trakee in one hand and gently stroked his head. "Yes, I think you are right. He will be a brave one. Come in and let us prepare him some food."

They took some corn meal and added goat's milk until it was mush. When Trakee awoke, they fed him small portions of the meal from their fingertips. He was soon full and fell asleep.

"He'll need to eat often," said Shakem. "You feed him through the nights and bring him by on your way to school. I will feed him in the day."

The next morning on the way to school, Akeem dropped Trakee off at his grandfather's house. Shakem had much to do, for this was the day that he went to trade at the river. Shakem took Trakee and placed him in a small basket. "Now, my son, hurry off to school and come quickly when class is done, for today we go to the tradesmen."

"I will, Grandfather," said Akeem as he picked up his knapsack and book.

When Akeem got to school, he could not keep his mind on his work. He loved to go trading. There were so many interesting people, and his grandfather loved to stop and talk. Most of all, Akeem loved the smell of the river, the fragrance stirred with adventure. Akeem's mind wandered.

Suddenly, he was a trader floating down the river in his canoe. Trakee, a grown leopard, sat in the back of the boat with a leather collar around his neck. Their cargo was ivory tusks from the Serengeti Plains. As he passed the other tradesmen, they tipped their hats or waved. They were in awe of this boy wonder who traveled with the wild leopard. Everyone wanted to trade with him, and he had amassed a great fortune.

As he drifted along, he spotted a herd of rhinoceros drinking at the water's edge. Akeem was watching white birds land on the backs of the rhinos, and he did not see the large crocodile as it entered the water and headed for his canoe. The crocodile rammed the canoe, knocking him back into the boat causing him to lose his oar into the murky water below.

Unshaken, he grabbed his spear and thrust it through the croc's back. The crocodile flipped and rolled in pain. He speared the creature again, this time on the underside. Blood changed the water's color to red. He grabbed the tail and quickly tied it with a rope to the back of his canoe. He would trade the hide and meat at his next port.

He sat back down in the canoe propped up his feet and leaned back on a sack of meal. He closed his eyes for a rest as he drifted down river.

Suddenly, Akeem's thoughts were interrupted by the bell, bringing him back from his daydream and sounding the end of the school day.

Akeem raced to his grandfather's. As he entered, he heard Trakee crying loudly. "That one's a good eater," said Shakem. "I've been pressed to get anything done except feed him. Here, it's your turn," smiled Shakem as he handed Akeem the bowl of mush.

Akeem picked up Trakee and fed him little bits of mush. Trakee was so small that it didn't take much to fill his stomach. This accounted for why he got hungry so often. Trakee closed his eyes and purred softly.

"You'd better put him down and help me load up or we will miss the tradesman." Akeem did as his grandfather asked.

Shakem made baskets and rugs out of dried reeds and strips of bark. He would load them up on his back once a week and trade them for the things he needed. As Akeem strapped on the last basket, Shakem called back, "You had better get the brave one and some mush. He'll be ready to eat again soon." Akeem grabbed the bowl of mush, cradled Trakee in the bend of his arm, and they were off to the river.

As they walked along, Shakem talked to Akeem, "You know, my son, God has a great plan for your life. He has much for you to do for Him."

"Grandfather, how do you know this? You have said this to me since I was a small boy. How do you know what God says?"

"He speaks to me."

"But how does He speak to you? Does He speak aloud like you and I?"

"He does at times speak aloud, but mostly He speaks to my mind. He is a calm and gentle voice in my mind."

"But Grandfather, how do you know they are not just your own thoughts?"

"Because I have learned to recognize His voice much like you have learned to recognize mine. If you are outside and I call your name, you know it is me. How? Because you know what my voice sounds like."

"But sometimes I hear thoughts in my head that are bad. Is that God?"

"No, if someone were imitating my voice, how would you know it was not me?"

"I would ask them a question only you and I know about."

"It is the same with God. He knows all about you and loves you more than I. His words will be consistent with who he is. He is love, so His words will be loving. He is truth, so His words will be truth. He is wise, so His words will guide you. He will tell you of things no one but you and He would know of."

"And will He tell me of this great purpose He has for me?"

"Ah, yes, He longs to speak to you of things to come, but also of things that are now. For instance, you know of the villagers I stop and talk to on trading days. Many times God will tell me words to encourage them or things I can do to help them. Only God knows what a man needs from day to day. Sometimes, what we think we need is not what we need at all."

"Grandfather, I want to learn to hear God's voice. Do you think I really can?"

"I am sure of it! He talks to anyone who will listen. If He will talk to me, He will talk to you."

As they continued walking, Akeem was silent. Inside, his thoughts were racing, "God, if You really do talk to people, I want You to talk to me. I know I am not perfect, but please teach me to hear You."

Before long, they were at the river. There were many people there today. Small canoes and dinghies lined the water's edge. "Good-aye, mate!" shouted a rough-looking man with ruffled, sandy blonde hair and a few day's growth of whiskers.

"Ah, how are you, my friend?" said Shakem as he made his way through the crowd and stuck out his hand in friendship. The men shook hands and greeted each other warmly. Akeem walked up behind his grandfather.

"Ah, and what do we have here, my lad, a baby leopard?" Akeem nodded *yes* as the man took Trakee in his hand.

This was Jack Henry, a high-spirited Australian man who had come to Africa to seek out adventure. He lived for three years on the plains hunting wild animals. He would trade their pelts for supplies and eat the meat for food.

Then, one day, Jack had been attacked by a lioness when he got too close to her cubs. He had wanted to see them up close and hold them. Tragically, Jack didn't see the lioness returning from her hunt. Jack escaped with his life, but lost his left hand. That was the end of his adventure seeking. He had settled down to a life of canoeing up and down the river trading wares.

Jack petted Trakee's head as he looked the cub over. Then suddenly, he shuddered as he said, "Can't say that I care for them cats much," and handed him back to Akeem. Shakem had put down his bundle and was busy untying it. "Now, my friend, what would you like to trade today?"

The men engaged in the usual trading conversation as Akeem took Trakee and milled through the crowd. The riverbank was filled with people; the smell of vegetables filled the air. Tradesmen chattered loudly as they bartered with the villagers. A merchant poured out a basket of old fish at the water's edge and several dogs rushed over to eat them. A woman merchant who was selling melons had cut one open and was handing out small bits for passersby to sample.

"What will I trade?" thought Akeem, "...baskets, tools, linens, chickens?" His thoughts were interrupted by a distressed, *Meow*! *Meow*!

"Okay, okay, I get the point." Akeem sat down on a wooden crate to feed Trakee. Just as he did, a chicken escaped from a bamboo cage, and a small woman with a turban on her head and a flock of young children behind her chased it wildly. Akeem watched the commotion as he fed Trakee. Several people stopped what they were doing to cheer the chicken on. Akeem couldn't help but smile. Finally, a man emerged from the crowd and caught the chicken for her. Akeem watched the people for several more minutes. Thinking his grandfather might need him, he made his way back to Jack's boat.

As he approached the two of them, they looked up from their work. "Akeem, your grandfather has been telling me of your dreams to become a tradesman. Maybe one day you can come work with me, eh?" Jack punched Akeem in the shoulder in a teasing sort of way. "I'll be needin' someone soon just to carry my bags of gold," he grinned.

Shakem held out his hand again to Jack, "Good bye, now, Jack."

"Good-aye, mate."

The men shook hands, and Shakem loaded up his back again, this time not with baskets, but with food he had traded for rice, beans, dried meat, corn... and in his hand a new knife for working.


Akeem and Shakem walked slowly back to the village. When they got to the outskirts of town, they were met with chaos. Men were running to and fro shouting commands at each other. Women and children clutched each other and cried. Akeem and Shakem looked at each other in bewilderment. A few feet away, Abaad Kimber, one of the villagers and a friend of Shakem's came racing by. Shakem caught him by the arm. "What is it, my friend?"

"Cave-in at the mine," said Abaad gravely, "there are men trapped."

Shakem's heart sank. Akeem felt tears come to his eyes. "Come now, my son, that won't do any good. Let us go see if we can be of some assistance." Shakem handed his bundle to Abaad as he and Akeem ran toward the mine.

# CHAPTER 3

—m—

The mine was just a mile outside of town and already a couple hundred people had gathered there. Men in hard hats were busy digging and removing debris. Women stood clutching each other weeping. The doctor from the local clinic and a few of his volunteers waited near the mouth of the mine with bags of medical supplies to treat the victims as they emerged. There were seventeen men still unaccounted for.

Akeem saw his mother and ran to her as fast as his legs could carry him. He threw his arms around her waist and hugged her. "Oh, Akeem, your father, I can't find him any-where!" They both sobbed uncontrollably.

Meanwhile, Shakem had rushed straight to the mouth of the mine to find William Stanton. He was the foreman, an African of British descent. Stanton's face was covered with black dirt, and he had cuts and scrapes on his arms. His shirt was torn, and he was drenched with sweat. His face was filled with worry and anxiety.

"What may I do to help?" asked Shakem, rolling up his sleeves.

"Get some water for the men working. They've been digging at a furious pace for the last hour and a half. I'm sure they are in need of a drink."

Stanton's eyes caught Shakem's. He looked sorrowful for a moment then quickly glanced down. "It's Dumaka, isn't it?" asked Shakem grasping Stanton's arm.

"Yes, Shakem, I'm afraid he's one of the men unaccounted for. I'm... I'm sorry," said Stanton, still looking down as he turned away.

Shakem's heart sank. His body went numb as his mind fought to pray. "Oh! God, no! Oh, my Father, please, no." Tears welled up in Shakem's eyes and spilled over onto his cheeks. Shakem stood still as the world rushed around him. "Oh, my God, my only son."

Such pain gripped his heart that he had never felt before. Grief and sorrow choked his breath, and for a few minutes his thoughts ran wild. Suddenly, he was brought back to reality by the shouting of the men digging in the mouth of the mine. They had found one of the men.

Two black men emerged from the mine carrying a third. He was cut badly on his shoulder, and his leg was broken. He gasped and coughed from the dust. The doctor ran to him as the two men laid him on a blanket on the ground.

"I have got to help," thought Shakem, and he ran to get water. He carried water back and forth for hours, giving drinks to the many working in and around the mine. During that time they found three more miners, but not Dumaka.

The sun began to set. Shakem made his way over to Akeem and Kamaria. Shakem hugged them both for a long time. He looked at Kamaria and said, "It's getting dark. Why don't you take the boy home and get some rest? Work will go slow in the darkness. I'll stay here and help."

Kamaria agreed, and the two quietly walked home with Trakee, the great African sun setting behind them.

Trakee cried all the way home. Akeem had dropped the bowl of mush while running to the mine so the cub was starving. Upon returning home, Akeem mixed up some meal and sat down at the table to feed him. Trakee purred as he licked it off Akeem's fingers.

Kamaria also went to the kitchen to prepare some food for them to eat. Kamaria had been in the process of preparing dinner when she heard of the cave-in. She had beans and rice in a pot all ready for cooking. "These will take several hours to cook. We can take them to the mine tomorrow and eat them cold," she thought, as she put them over a low fire.

Then she took a loaf of bread she had baked earlier that day and sliced off several slices for her and Akeem. She had picked a small melon from her garden, which she cut into wedges and placed on the table by the bread. Kamaria put water on to boil, and she took out some tea leaves and spooned some into a small earthen pitcher. She set the pitcher on the stove. Then she went to the shelf to get two mugs and placed them on the table. She sat down exhausted and stared off into a corner.

Trakee had eaten his fill, and Akeem had wrapped him in a cloth for the night and laid him down. The water on the stove was boiling. Akeem looked at his mother. She looked worried and worn from the day's events. His heart went out to her. He went to the stove and poured the hot water into the pitcher, then brought the pitcher to the table and sat down. "Mama, are you ready to pray?" Kamaria bowed her head and quietly cried.

"Dear God," began Akeem, "please help them find Father. Help him not to be afraid. Help Mama not to worry, God. Help her sleep tonight. Amen."

Akeem looked at his mother. She sat, head bowed, wiping her tears. Akeem poured her some tea and helped himself to some bread and melon. Kamaria lifted her head, and began to sip her tea slowly as she stared blankly at the wall. Akeem did not know what to say to her, so he ate in silence. When he finished, he kissed his mother and went to bed.

The next morning Kamaria was up early. She had not slept well. She stirred the beans and rice and then scooped out enough for herself, Akeem and Shakem and placed them in a clay bowl and wrapped it with a cloth. She took several slices of bread and wrapped them in a small cloth also. She put both these and the remaining melon in a gunnysack to take to the mine. She also put in some spoons and a cup.

Akeem walked in sleepy-eyed. He hugged his mother and sat down. She poured him some warm goat's milk and gave him some cornbread that she had baked that morning. She sat down with a piece for herself and a cup of tea. They ate quietly until Trakee woke up.

"I'll feed him," said Kamaria as she patted Akeem's arm. "You finish eating." Kamaria got the cub and mixed him some meal. Then she put some in a cup to take with them. When everyone had finished eating, they set out for the mine.

By the time they arrived, there were already fresh crews working to get the trapped men out. Shakem had fallen asleep for a couple of hours during the night but was back up assisting anywhere he could. Kamaria went over to talk to him. "Any news yet?" she asked hopeful.

"No, my child," he said grimly. "They have been working all night. They have tunneled through about thirty feet but still have not found an opening."

"You look tired, Shakem. I brought you some food."

"Thank you, I am very hungry."

Kamaria opened the sack and gave food to Shakem. Kamaria and Akeem sat with Shakem as he ate. Shakem wanted to enjoy his meal, but instead felt guilty for eating, knowing his son had not eaten for many hours. Akeem let Trakee down. He played around them batting their knees and feet with his paws.

"He seems to be fattening up a bit," said Shakem.

"Yes, his stomach is getting round," answered Akeem. "Did we remember food for him?"

Kamaria nodded *yes*. She looked up and saw a friend whose husband was also missing. "I'm going to go talk to Neema," she said as she got up.

Neema sat nursing her baby. She and her husband Moswen had only been married a little over a year. As Kamaria approached her she could see Neema's eyes were full of tears. Neema looked up and saw Kamaria walking over. Neema tried to dry her eyes but it was no use.

Kamaria hugged her and Neema burst into tears. Kamaria hugged tighter and rocked her gently. "I know, I know," said Kamaria. The two sat clutched for several minutes. Then Kamaria sat back.

Neema moved her now sleeping baby down onto her lap. She wiped her face again on her robe. "What am I going to do? What am I going to do?" said Neema, not expecting an answer.

Kamaria felt for her. Although she had Akeem and knew she would be the only parent and sole provider if they didn't find Dumaka, her heart went out to Neema. Her baby was only a few weeks old. It would be much harder for her to try to work and take care of the baby, too.

"What have you heard?" asked Kamaria, trying to catch Neema's eyes.

"They found two more men last night.... They didn't make it."

Kamaria's heart sank. She realized Shakem knew this but had kept it from her. She was glad for Akeem's sake. She searched for words of consolation.

"God, I know I have no need to fear, but I feel so alone," she prayed silently.

"*KAMARIA, HE WHO KEEPS YOU WILL NOT SLUMBER*," she heard in her mind. She knew it was God. She repeated it aloud.

"Neema, He who keeps you will not slumber. The Lord will take care of us." Neema knew this, but she still needed to hear it. She kissed her little one's round soft cheek. Tears trickled down her cheeks again. Her eyes hurt. She had cried most of the night. Kamaria, sensing this, took the baby and made a soft pile of clothes by Neema. "Here, you lay your head on these and rest a little. I'll take care of her." Neema did lie down and was soon asleep.

She slept for a few hours and would have probably kept on sleeping had the baby not started crying. Neema sat up groggy and wiped her eyes. "I'll take her," she said as she took her baby to nurse her. "Did I sleep long?"

Kamaria nodded, "A few hours."

"I'm sorry."

"Don't apologize. You needed it very badly."

Kamaria was right. Sleep was the only thing that brought relief from the torturous waiting. She wished she could sleep.

Suddenly, there was a commotion over in front of the mine. People ran close to see what was happening. Akeem and his grandfather had been giving drinks to the workers close by. Akeem dropped his water jug and ran as fast as he could to his mother. "Mother, mother," shouted Akeem breathlessly as he fell at his mother's side, "they've broken through! They found a space where there are no rocks!"

Kamaria felt limp. "Oh, thank You, God." She thought to herself.

Akeem grabbed her by the arm. "Come on, Mother, come on!"

Kamaria got up, and they ran to the mine. Soon the crowd was so thick around the mouth of the mine that people were being pushed and shoved. Stanton, the foreman, stood on a pile of rocks and waved his arms to get the multitude's attention. The noise died down only slightly as people whistled and shushed each other. Then the crowd grew quiet.

"We have found a clearing," shouted Stanton, trying to speak loud enough for everyone to hear. The noise of the mass of people rose again as many began to talk to each other. Stanton waived his arms again. Someone whistled loudly. When everyone was silent he began again.

"We have found a clearing. However, the hole is too small for anyone to get through. We are in the process of widening it right now. We are asking that everyone go back to the place they were waiting. The noise is too loud, and we cannot hear if any of the trapped men are calling out. Please go back and sit down. We will let you know of any progress." The swarm began to break up as people scuffled back to their places.

It seemed as if hours had gone by, when in fact, it had only been about forty minutes. People were beginning to feel antsy when suddenly men covered in dirt emerged from the mine. It was three of the missing miners and one of the workmen.

The great expanse of people rose to their feet and started for the mine. Stanton climbed up on a rock again yelling, "Please do not move toward the mine unless you have medical training. I repeat, please do not move toward the mine unless you have medical training."

A handful of individuals made their way up to the quarry. They promptly began examining the newly exca-vated miners. Several more men appeared in the cavity. Then two laborers emerged from the mine carrying another man. A total of twelve had been found. There were still five missing.

As the men emerged, Neema recognized Moswen. She picked up her baby and raced to him. She kissed his dirty face and squeezed him tightly. Her tears wet the soot on his face leaving clean streaks behind.

Kamaria was relieved. She loved Neema and Moswen and was truly happy for them. She hurried over to join the others in their celebration. She wandered from one med-ical site to another looking for Dumaka. She did not find him. The men who were not badly wounded were treated, and the reunited families returned home.

The work continued well into the evening. They had found a chasm about thirty feet long in which these men had been trapped. But then the tunnel ended again in an insurmountable pile of rubble. Kamaria and Akeem stayed until sunset. With each passing day they knew the chances of finding Dumaka alive diminished. They were dirty and tired as they walked home speaking of other's restorations, trying to sound hopeful for one another.


When they arrived home, Akeem went and washed. He readied himself for bed and joined his mom in the kitchen. Kamaria was trying to make something that they could take to the mine the next day to eat. She had warmed some cornbread and milk and left it on the table for Akeem. Akeem entered the room and asked, "Mom, do you hear God?"

Kamaria, too deep in thought, did not answer.

"Mom... Mom... Mom..."

Kamaria broke her glazed looked and answered, "What, Akeem?"

"Do you hear God?"

"Yes, yes, I do," Kamaria answered quickly and to the point. She was worried and did not feel like talking. She turned and slipped back into her thoughts.

"What does God sound like?"

"What?" Kamaria stumbled trying to loose her mind from the pictures that raced around her head. "Uh, well... well, His voice is gentle and soothing. It sort of warms me inside." As Kamaria spoke of God's voice, clarity began to come back to her thinking.

"It's peaceful and brings calmness to my heart and my mind." She laughed half-heartedly. "Peace and calmness - that's what I need," she thought.

"Have you always heard God, Mother?"

"Well, actually," said Kamaria as she pulled out a chair and sat down at the table with Akeem, "it took me a couple of years to really be sure of His voice, but once I began asking Him to speak to me, I found that He had been speaking to me all my life, but I didn't know how to listen."

"What does He say?"

"He speaks to me of many things. I write His words down in a book and keep them. When I am in distress, He speaks calmness. When I am disobedient, He is firm and corrects me. When I don't know what to do, He guides me in life."

Kamaria rubbed Akeem's arm gently. "Thank you, child," she said with a smile.

"For what?" asked Akeem.

"For reminding me where my peace comes from."

They kissed good night. Kamaria went to bathe and Akeem went on to bed. Akeem lay awake in bed for a long time that night. He was scared and anxious. He prayed earnestly for God to keep his dad alive. He prayed that God would speak to him. He cried for his father and finally fell asleep.

# CHAPTER 4

—⁐⁓—

Shakem sat against a rock, his strength depleted. It had been two and a half days since he had first come to the mine. He had not been home since. As he sat in the darkness illuminated only by a small campfire at the mouth of the mine, a lantern sitting atop a mound of rocks, and the stars above, Shakem prayed once again for his son.

"Father God, I know You are a loving God. I know You love Dumaka more than I. Please do not take him. Please do not take my only son," Shakem cried. Then realizing his prayers might be too late added, "God, if You have to take him, please let us find his body so that we may bury him properly."

Shakem leaned his head back and drifted off to sleep. A few hours passed. Shakem had a dream.

He dreamt he was inside the mine with the workmen. He was wearing a metal hard hat with a light on it. The light would shine on different areas of the shaft depending on where he turned his head. The workmen in front of him stood in front of a small opening atop of a mound of rock and debris. They were motioning for him to go through the hole. He had to climb up the pile and scoot his body through. When he got through to the other side he waited for the search party. After the other men joined him, they proceeded down the long dark tunnel.

One of the search men yelled to see if anyone would answer. They came to a split in the tunnel. The group divided; half the men went to the left, and Shakem along with the other half, went to the right. The tunnel narrowed and turned, then made a sharp downward slope.

There were large boxes on wheels full of rough diamonds and dirt. Shovels and picks were strewn about. There was a lunch box opened with a half-eaten sandwich lying next to it. A blue jean jacket lay in a heap. The men in front of Shakem stopped. One of them thought he had heard something. The men listened intently. They heard it again. It sounded like a very muffled cough.

The men hurried on. There was debris scattered all around which made running an impossibility. They soon came to another blockage. A large beam had broken loose from the rafters and lay with one end still attached to the ceiling and one end on the ground. Dirt and rocks had fallen from above and filled the cavity. Once again, they heard a cough.

Shakem awoke suddenly. He was startled to find he had been dreaming. The pictures he had seen were so real. He was sure this tunnel must be where Dumaka was. If only the workmen could get through that blockage he would be able to show them where to go. Shakem got up and ran over to the campfire. Most of the men around the fire were asleep.

Stanton felt that he should be awake for the men that were working, should they need anything, so he had been sleeping very little. Shakem sat down beside him. Stanton offered him some coffee. Shakem took it thankfully. "Have they burrowed through yet?" asked Shakem.

"Not yet, but a fresh crew went to work about an hour ago."

Stanton picked up a stick and poked the fire. There was a pack of hyenas prowling in the distance. They could sense something was injured and death was lurking close by. They wanted to move in closer but the fire kept them at bay.

"I've had a dream. I know where they are."

Stanton looked at Shakem surprised, and then added, "With every passing hour their chances of survival diminishes. We need all the help we can get. I may catch slack for this but when they break through, would you like to go in with the men?"

Shakem answered, "Yes."

All night, the men worked in the tunnel. Finally, around daybreak there was shouting from the shaft. They had made it through. Shakem was relieved but knew they would soon come to another blockage.

The men sleeping around the fire stirred. The sun was coming up, and it was their turn in the mine. The women from the village had brought out some food the day before for the workers. There were a couple of loaves of bread left. The men divided this and ate it with their coffee and went to work in the mine.

The men who had been working all night got themselves water to drink and rinsed their faces. A couple of them drank coffee. They wanted to stay awake to see if the men were found, but they also knew they needed to go sleep in case they were called upon again.

Shakem joined the new shift of men in the mine. The going was slow. Although they had been tunneling for two days, there was much debris all through the tunnels. The route to the latest breakthrough was challenging at best.

The rescue team trudged on. Finally, they came to the opening. Shakem watched as the first workmen wriggled through the gap. A second workman waived Shakem on through the small opening. He climbed through to the other side. The first workman was yelling to see if anyone would answer. No one did.

The rest of the party joined them as they continued down the cool dark shaft. Just as in Shakem's dream, they came to a fork in the tunnel where it split. The man in charge of the rescue team began dividing them and Shakem immediately motioned to him that he would follow the second group to the right. The tunnel had grown progressively more cluttered. They were now continually climbing up and over debris. Soon, they came to another complete blockage. Two of the men turned back to go get more help while Shakem and the remaining miner began excavating.

They picked a large wooden beam and laid it along the side of the tunnel out of the way. Then one by one they removed large rocks and made a pile of them off to the side. The other man yelled. They waited... no response. They worked diligently. Eventually, six more workmen joined them. They dug and hauled off rocks and broken beams for hours.

Another man came down the shaft carrying a large pitcher of water. Everyone stopped working and got a refreshing drink.

"I heard something!" said one of the men. They all strained to hear even the faintest of sounds. They waited. One man moved and started to talk. They all shushed him.

Then they heard it. A muffled cough. They had found someone. Shakem's heart raced. "Oh God, please let that be Dumaka. Please let him be all right."

The men continued to dig. Finally, they broke through! They shouted through the hole, which was about the size of a man's fist. Someone called back, "We're in here! We're in here!"

The men dug at a frantic pace. Soon the opening was large enough for someone to get through. The smallest man crawled through. It was silent for a couple a minutes. It seemed like an eternity. "I've found them. They're here! They are all here!"

The workmen on the other side shouted and hugged one another. Shakem asked if he could go through next. He put his feet through and then pulled his body. A sharp rock scraped his side. He dropped to the ground as his head cleared the opening. It was pitch black. He had the others hand him his hard hat with the light. He put it on and looked around the cavern. As he stumbled along the pathway, he heard voices ahead.

His heart was pounding and he hurried to move through, but then fell down. He picked himself up and pushed on. He finally saw a light ahead. He prayed intently, "Oh God, please God, please let him be all right."

Shakem could see figures. He worked his way toward them. It was a workman and one of the missing miners. He was hurt badly. Shakem looked around the shaft; he saw two more men lying a few feet away. He rushed to them. One man groaned as he moved debris off him. The other man lay face down with a large beam across his back.

Shakem pulled the beam to the side and turned the man over. It was Dumaka. He was dead.

Shakem screamed, "No... no! Oh God, not my Dumaka!" Shakem hugged him and cried. He picked up his upper body and held him in his lap.

"Oh, my Dumaka. Oh my son. No, not my son! No, not my son!" He rocked him and wept.

"Oh God, why did he have to die! What will we do without him? What will Kamaria and Akeem do without him?"

They found the last two men. One was in a coma, and the other had died. Word spread quickly through the crowd outside. Stanton told Kamaria and Akeem of Dumaka's death.

They were crying and holding each other while others around them tried to comfort them. Shakem came to them. He hugged them, and they all wept great, deep tears.

Finally Kamaria broke the silence, "We had better go home". Shakem nodded *yes*.

"I'll be right back," he added. Shakem found Stanton. He held out his hand to him. "Thank you for all you did to find them."

Stanton shook Shakem's hand and then grabbed him. They squeezed each other tightly. Both men cried. "I'm so sorry Shakem. I can't imagine your loss. I'm so sorry." Shakem shook his head in acceptance. Their eyes barely caught each other as Shakem turned to walk away.

They walked in silence all the way home. When they got to Shakem's house, Kamaria asked him to come over later that afternoon. Shakem agreed, hugged them both goodbye, and went inside.

Kamaria and Akeem walked wearily toward their home. They were exhausted both physically and emotionally. When they arrived home, their house was still. There was a quiet emptiness and a lifelessness that hung heavy in the air. Kamaria cried tears she didn't think she had left. Akeem sat limply next to her.

"We had better rest. Akeem, feed Trakee and then lay down."

"Yes, Mother," said Akeem with no emotion. Kamaria went to her room and closed the door. Akeem fed Trakee and started to put him in his basket, and then he changed his mind and took the cub to bed with him.

They slept for several hours. When Kamaria awoke she thought about Dumaka and what had transpired that day. Tears swelled in her eyes. She wanted to go back to sleep. She wanted to wake up and find that it was all a bad dream. She breathed a deep sigh, then climbed out of bed and washed her face.

She went out in the garden and gathered some pumpkin leaves in a basket and picked a couple of squash. She brought them inside and washed and prepared them. She scrubbed some potatoes and put them on to boil. Then she mixed some cornbread and put it in the oven.

Shakem knocked at the door and opened it without waiting for an answer. He came into the kitchen and sat down at the table. Kamaria said hello and turned again to her cooking. The two didn't have much to say. The shock of the day's events left them quiet.

Akeem came in carrying Trakee. Once again, it was feeding time. Akeem hugged his grandfather and sat down at the table with Trakee and his food. Shakem watched as the cub licked the meal hungrily. "Ouch!" yipped Akeem. "He bit me!"

Kamaria turned and looked at him then grinned at Shakem. Akeem and Shakem smiled, too. It felt good to smile. "Maybe he's getting big enough to eat out of the bowl," said Shakem.

Akeem put the bowl on the table then set Trakee next to it and pushed his nose into it. Trakee sneezed and backed up a couple of steps. He licked his paw and washed his face. Then he stepped up to the bowl again and cautiously sniffed the meal. Once again, he got some up his nose and sneezed. He licked the meal with his tiny pink tongue and then stopped to wash his face. He repeated this process over a couple more times then, seemingly full, he stumbled over to Akeem.

"He certainly knows who takes care of him," said Shakem. Akeem stroked his fur, and Trakee purred and licked his hand. "He sure is a young one to be without his mother and father," said Shakem. His words hung in the air, he wished he could take them back. He looked at Akeem. He too was young to be without his father.

He rubbed Akeem's head. "I love you, Akeem."

"I love you, too, Grandfather."

Kamaria's eyes filled with tears again.

Soon dinner was cooked. Kamaria put food on their plates and set them on the table. They bowed their heads to pray. Shakem prayed aloud, "Oh God, You are a good God. Lord, we don't understand Your ways. Thank You for letting us find Dumaka. Help us to understand why You took him. Lead us and guide us. Be with Kamaria and Akeem during this difficult time, protect them and provide for them. We ask these things in the name of Jesus. Amen."

During dinner they talked of funeral plans. They would ask four of Dumaka's friends from the mine to carry the coffin- one of which would be Moswen. The preacher from their mission would say a few words.

They talked well into the evening. "I'll need to get a job," said Kamaria. "Would you mind watching Akeem while I work?"

"Of course," answered Shakem. "What kind of work will you look for?"

"I'm not sure. I haven't worked since Akeem was born."

"You will figure it out," said Shakem as he squeezed her hand. "I had better go now."

Shakem got up and went into Akeem's room. Akeem was lying on his bed holding Trakee. Shakem sat on the bed next to Akeem. "Akeem, you are not alone. God is here, ready to help you and speak to you."

Akeem shook his head *yes*. Shakem kissed his forehead and went home.

Akeem lay in his bed awake for quite a while. He ached inside a big, deep indescribable ache. He closed his eyes, "God, why did You take my dad? Why did he have to die? Please, can't You make him come back? Please God, please bring him back!"

Akeem rolled over and buried his face in the pillow and wept. He cried for what seemed like hours; his eyes burned. His entire being was exhausted. He had nothing in him but tears, and yet he knew tears would not change things.

Akeem remembered his grandfather telling him God would speak to him. He wiped his eyes and blew his nose. He rolled back over onto his back and closed his eyes. "God, I know You are real. I need You to talk to me. I don't know how to hear Your voice. But God, I really need You to talk to me. I feel so alone, so helpless. Please talk to me, God. Please, God!"

Akeem lay still. He quieted his mind and stopped thinking. Then he heard a comforting thought. "I will never leave you or forsake you." Akeem knew this. It was a Bible verse he had learned from his grandfather. "I am your Father. I will never leave you or forsake you. You are not abandoned. You are not an orphan. You are a child of the king. Therefore, you are a prince... Prince Akeem."

Akeem cried again, he realized how very much God loved him and how very thankful he was for that love. He also knew that for the very first time, he had heard God's voice. He felt very peaceful and slept soundly that night.

The next day was the funeral. Kamaria had spent much of the morning making preparations. She had gone to the river to get flowers, and arranged the details with friends and loved ones. That afternoon people gathered at the mission. Many of their friends were there. They offered words of consolation to them.

Jack Stanton and many of the men from the mine were there also. The other miners who had died were being buried today too. The crowd was rather large. The coffins were plain wood boxes, but people had covered them with fresh flowers. Akeem was very grieved over his father, but he felt different today. Somehow, today he had hope... something he didn't have the day before. He wasn't exactly sure why, but he didn't carry the same feeling of devastation anymore.

Akeem's pastor arrived. People stilled and shuffled into place. The pastor said a few words, and then the men lifted the coffins up on their shoulders. Many of the people carried flowers; others had Bibles or crying cloths. The crowd walked slowly down the dusty road through town. Shop owners and customers came out of the wooden, hut-like buildings and stood in respect as the procession passed by. Women buying fruit and vegetables from stands stopped and gazed sorrowfully. Little children ran out to see the bright colored flowers and hear the singing.

Slowly, the procession made its way through town to the graveyard. The coffins were set in a row and the pastor prayed over them. He prayed for the wives and children left behind. They sang some songs, and people walked up and placed more flowers on and around the coffins. They prayed for a while longer at the gravesite and then went home. Friends and families they knew came over to their house and brought food. People talked of Dumaka and what a good man he was and how much he would be missed.

It was a long afternoon. Both Kamaria and Akeem felt relieved as people began to trickle out. Neema and Moswen were among the last to leave. It was early evening by the time the food was cleaned up and everyone had gone.

Only Shakem had stayed. The three of them sat talking of the day's events and how helpful everyone had been. Many of the ladies had left food for them and offered to help take care of Akeem. One of the men had told Kamaria to come see him about a job. The pastor had given her money that the mission had collected for them the day before.

Kamaria made coffee for her and Shakem. She poured milk for Akeem and brought their drinks to them in the living room. They sat quietly as they drank their drinks. Kamaria broke the silence. "Akeem, I got you something today while I was at the tradesman's," she said as she went into her bedroom. She came out with a small book and handed it to Akeem. Akeem opened it. The pages were blank except for lines. Akeem had never seen a book with no words in it. Puzzled, he looked at his mother.

"This book is for you to write down the words God speaks to you so you will always have them and will be able to see His faithfulness." Akeem had not told his mother that God had spoken to him the night before. He hugged his mom and told her thank you.

Later that night, when Akeem was in his room, he opened the book from his mother. He prayed over the book. He asked God to fill it with His words for him. He wrote down all that God had said to him the night before. Then Akeem lay on his bed and prayed. Again, he heard God speak to him in his mind. "I am always with you. I am never far off. Look for Me at school. Listen for Me in the market. I have a great call and a destiny for you. You must always keep looking and listening for Me."

Akeem lay in bed awake a long time reading over God's words to him. He wondered what God's plan for him was. He stroked Trakee who was lying nestled in his armpit purring. He read and finally drifted off to sleep.

The months passed. Kamaria started working for a clothing mill. Akeem was now out of school for the summer and was spending his days with his grandfather. The two were out behind Shakem's house. The sun was hot and merciless. Shakem and Akeem were hoeing weeds in Shakem's garden. The weather was very dry and the vegetables and fruits he had planted didn't need any competition for the water.

Akeem bent over to pull a large thistle weed. He put both hands around the stalk and pulled hard. The roots gave way, and he fell over backward onto Trakee. Trakee yipped and batted at Akeem.

"I'm sorry, Trakee," said Akeem, holding out his hand to him. Trakee licked his back foot and then took his time walking over to Akeem. Akeem leaned over to pet him. He was not a baby anymore. His head was up to Akeem's knee. He rubbed his head on Akeem's leg and purred loudly.

"You two had better get some work done. We'll be lucky to get to the tradesman at this rate," said Shakem. Akeem gave Trakee's ear a tug and went back to hoeing. They continued working long into the morning.

When they were finally done, the three went into the cool of the house and got a drink of water. They made a lunch of boiled vegetables and tea. Then they rested for a while and talked of their plans for the afternoon.

Later that afternoon, as they walked the dusty road to the river, Trakee lagged behind and batted at moths and bugs. Shakem and Akeem had to wait for him several times to catch up. Finally, when Akeem could take it no more he scolded him, "Trakee, if you stop one more time I'm going to start leaving you home." Trakee looked at him with his head tilted as if he was really listening. Then he ran up to Akeem and bounded on him playfully. "No kidding," said Akeem giggling. "You better straighten up... I mean it." Trakee licked Akeem's face furiously and purred.

"We are never going to get there like this," said Shakem smiling at the two of them. Akeem pushed Trakee off and stood up. They continued on toward the river stopping every few minutes to let Trakee catch up. When they finally did arrive, the docks were very crowded. Akeem tied a small rope around Trakee's neck to keep him from getting lost. They wove their way through the swarming crowd to Jack Henry's canoe.

Two of Shakem's friends from the village were there. They all greeted each other. "That leopard is really growing," said Jack to Akeem. "You gonna turn him loose soon?"

Akeem's heart sank. He had always known that he would one day have to turn Trakee back to the wild, but Jack's comment made it suddenly seem all too real. "I don't know," said Akeem, shrugging his shoulders. The thought saddened Akeem. He listened to the others talking but sat quietly holding back his emotions. The men were joking and laughing.

Shakem saw Akeem and knew that Jack's statement had hurt him. He wanted to cheer him up. "You know, once a long time ago," started Shakem.... The others grew quiet and settled themselves to listen. They had known Shakem a long time and could tell when he was beginning one of his stories....

"There was once a brave warrior named Trakee. He was the son of one of our ancestral kings. Every day, Prince Trakee and the other warriors from his tribe would go to the bush to hunt and practice their spear throwing. One day, while they were chasing a wild boar, warriors from a tribe to the north sneaked up on them. They waited in silence and watched Trakee and his men.

"Then their evil leader, King Java, sounded the war cry. A fierce battle took place. Screams and death cries filled the air. They were fighting hard and furiously. Prince Trakee had slain three warriors by himself. He was wrestling with another warrior when suddenly King Java was over him. Java raised his spear and proclaimed, 'I will kill the prince. Leave him to me.'

"With that, the other warrior picked up his weapon and quickly resumed the battle. Java stood over Prince Trakee; hate filled his eyes. 'I have waited a long time for this. I have warred with your father for many years. Now, I will take what means the most to him... his son.' Java's hands tightened as he raised the spear back ready to thrust it through the Prince.

"Then, just as Java was about to thrust the spear, he was knocked hard to the ground. The spear missed the Prince. Prince Trakee heard the screams of Java, thinking that it was one of his tribesmen that had knocked the deadly warrior off his feet. He looked over and gasped when he saw a leopard tearing at Java. Prince Trakee held his breath as he watched.

"The Prince heard the sounds of war behind him and suddenly remembered his fellow tribesmen. He got up and ran to help another in fight. The battle went on for several more minutes. When the last of the warring tribe had fled, the Prince and his men went to gather their wounded. Many a brave man was lost that day.

"Prince Trakee walked over to where Java lay. He looked at him dead on the ground and thought of the leopard that had saved his life. 'How odd for a wild animal to get involved in one of man's battles,' he thought.

"As he stood there, his eyes caught something moving in the distance. It was the leopard standing about forty feet away, looking at him. The two stared at each other for a long minute. The Prince broke the silence, 'You have saved me. I will not forget this. You and your sons will always find protection with me and my sons. We will not hunt you or your offspring. I make a pact with you, my friend.'

"And with that, the leopard turned and disappeared once again into the bush. Prince Trakee looked down at Java again and then joined the other warriors on the journey home. And so it is that Prince Trakee's descendants even to this day are friends with the leopard."

The men smiled at Shakem's story and began shaking hands, finishing their trades for the day. With a warmness in his heart, Akeem turned to pet his beloved Trakee, and found the leopard staring back at him with a knowing gaze.

# CHAPTER 5

—⁓—

As the weeks passed, Akeem would lie in bed at night and pray. He would often write in his journal God's words. Every night, he would ask God to show him his destiny and what His plan for him was.

One afternoon, as he and Trakee were walking to his grandfather's house, Trakee slapped at Akeem's heel as he often did. The two chased each other playfully. Akeem would grab at his tail, and in turn Trakee would spin and jump at him. This went on for several minutes. Akeem took Trakee by the ears and wrestled him to the ground.

Trakee reacted quickly, nipping Akeem on the hand. Akeem jerked his hand back in pain. Trakee had sliced open Akeem's palm. It was a bad cut. Trakee butted his head on Akeem's back and bounded around to the front. Akeem's hand hurt badly.

"No Trakee, you hurt me!" snapped Akeem. Trakee did not understand. Akeem stood up and called Trakee to follow him. His hand was bleeding severely. He hurried home and got a strip of cloth to wrap his hand. The bandage was soon covered with blood. Akeem unwrapped it and put on a fresh cloth.

Akeem sat with Trakee for a long time. He knew Trakee had grown much too large to keep. School was starting back soon and Trakee was too big to be left alone. His heart ached. Trakee was his best friend. He tried to think of some way he could continue to keep him. He knew he could not.

Akeem went to the kitchen and poured himself a cup of goat's milk. He put some in a bowl and set it on the floor for Trakee. "Trakee!" he called. Trakee came and licked up the milk quickly. Akeem drank his milk then reluctantly went to his room to get Trakee's rope and the little bit of money he had. He tied the rope around Trakee's neck and the two of them walked toward the town.

Trakee was now well past Akeem's knees in height and weighed between sixty to seventy pounds. As they walked along, Akeem remembered finding Trakee. How frightened and helpless he was! Tears filled Akeem's eyes, and he choked them back. He wished he could keep him forever.

When they got to the main road through town, Akeem made his way to the butcher. He walked up to the outside stand. There were live chickens in bamboo cages. Sides of pork hung by the foot from ropes. Fish lay in baskets their eyes staring coldly. Akeem waited as the butcher traded a woman some fish for a basket of vegetables she had grown.

Then the man turned to Akeem. "What do you want young man?"

"I'd like to buy a chicken." The man bent down and unlatched a cage. He grabbed a chicken as it squawked wildly. Then he latched the cage and turned the chicken upside down. He tied twine around the chicken's feet and handed it to Akeem.

Akeem paid the butcher and started down the dirt road toward the river. The chicken was flapping about, and this made Trakee very frisky. Several times he batted at the chicken. Each time Akeem would lift the chicken high above Trakee's head and give him a firm, "No."

About halfway between town and the river, Akeem turned off and walked into the bush. The dry weeds were about waist high as they pushed their way deep into the bush. Finally, when Akeem could no longer see the road, he stopped. He knelt down to look into Trakee's face holding the chicken high with one arm. He rubbed Trakee's fur and kissed his furry face. Trakee was completely distracted by the chicken and did not realize that Akeem was telling him goodbye.

He choked as he spoke to Trakee. "Now, be careful; don't go poking your nose down snake holes or running in front of the elephants. You've got to be careful. It's dangerous out here."

Akeem hugged Trakee again. "Here you go, boy," he said as he untied the chicken and turned it loose. Trakee, overcome with the excitement of it all, chased after the chicken. Trakee never noticed that his best friend had turned and walked away, leaving the leopard to live in the wild somewhere on the plains of Africa.

That night his mother washed and dressed his wound. Akeem went to his room and shut the door. He missed Trakee and felt sick in his stomach, much like he did when his dad had died. Akeem cried. He got mad at God. "Why do You take everything I love? Why does life have to hurt so much! Why, God? Can't something turn out right?"

Akeem cried and cried. He had bitterness and resentment against God for his dad dying. "You could have saved him, God, if You cared, You would have saved him. You're nothing but a big fake! You're not even real!"

Akeem knew that he didn't mean what he said, but he was speaking from his heart, and his heart felt like a big open sore which still hadn't healed. He felt like he needed an operation to take out the bitterness, an operation which he knew deep down that only God could do.

The next day Akeem went to his grandfather's house. He was still mad at God, and because of this he was very cross. He sat down on a chair with a scowl on his face and kicked at a clay pot sitting near him. The pot toppled over but didn't break.

Shakem turned, "Akeem, what are you doing? That took me hours to make." Shakem frowned at Akeem as he set the pot up. Akeem got up with his arms folded and shuffled his way across the room. "Akeem, son, God does not want you to act this way," said Shakem.

"I don't care what God wants!" shouted Akeem as he burst into tears and slumped to the floor hiding his face in his hands. Shakem was startled. He knew there was something seriously wrong for Akeem to act this way. He sat beside him on the floor and put his arm around him.

"Do you really mean that, Akeem?"

"Yes!" he shouted back.

Shakem knew from experience that someone so angry at God was likely talking out of deep hurt and disappointment.

"You are mad at God?"

"Yes!" snapped Akeem.

"And what are you mad at Him about?"

"He took my dad, and now I had to give up Trakee, and I don't have anyone!"

Shakem put the other arm around Akeem and hugged him for several minutes. Shakem prayed under his breath. "God show me what You want me to do or say." Shakem sat quietly and listened for God. "I am the great healer and restorer. Bring him back to his memory of the day his father died."

"Yes, God," prayed Shakem silently.

"Akeem, God wants to talk to you about your dad. Will you let Him?" asked Shakem.

Akeem wiped his face. He was still very mad. "Why?"

"Because as long as we are looking at things from our point of view, we cannot see the truth. God wants to show us things from His point of view to bring us freedom," said Shakem.

Akeem sat thinking about it for a few moments, and then half-heartedly muttered "ok," as he wiped his face again.

"Akeem, close your eyes," began Shakem, "I want you to picture your dad at the mine working just before the collapse."

Akeem did this. "Now, ask Jesus to show you your father's death from His point of view."

Akeem prayed, "Jesus, show me dad's death from Your point of view." Tears trickled down his cheeks as he prayed.

Akeem could see his father in the mine working and talking to the other miners. He had dirt on his face, and he was sweating. Suddenly, there was a rumble and the mine collapsed. Dust was everywhere. His father lay flat on his face with a big beam across his back. He was breathing hard and praying for God to help him.

"I can see him! I can see father, and he needs help!" said Akeem aloud. Then Akeem saw a dark figure lurking beside his father. He knew it was evil. It knelt beside Dumaka and grinned. Then it took a big sucking breath and, as it did, it pulled all the life out of Dumaka.

Akeem said aloud, "Jesus, weren't You there?" With his eyes still closed, he saw a bright light in the mine. It was Jesus. He was standing a few feet away from Dumaka. He looked at Dumaka with sadness in His eyes. Akeem thought Jesus looked like he wanted to go comfort his dad.

Then Jesus glared at the evil shadow. He pointed to the dark figure and said, "I command you to go!" Jesus walked over to Dumaka and kneeled over him. He stroked his hand and, as He did, great drops of His blood dripped onto Dumaka. Jesus prayed, "Father, I have not lost one that You have given to Me."

With this, Dumaka stirred. Then he opened his eyes and sat up. He was surrounded by a bright light and dressed in white linen. He was startled, and looked at Jesus as He helped him get up. Then Jesus said, "You are alive. Dumaka, you will live with Me in eternity forever, and there is no one that can prevent that."

Akeem opened his eyes. He almost couldn't believe what he had seen, but he knew it was real... in his heart. All the anger and resentment he had felt toward God was gone. He knew who had taken his father away, and it wasn't God. Akeem wiped his tears again. He felt so relieved and free! All those months he had been carrying so much bitterness toward God.

Akeem prayed, "God, I'm sorry for blaming You for my dad's death. I didn't understand. Please forgive me. Please help me to always see things from Your point of view."

Then he began to pray aloud, "God, I know it's not Your fault that Trakee got too big and I had to turn him loose. Please take care of him, God. Please keep him safe and make sure he gets enough to eat. He really likes chickens, so send an especially fat one his way. And make sure he finds friends to frolic and play with... and God, sometime; will You let me see him again? Amen."

Shakem began to chuckle at his prayer. Akeem looked at his grandfather. His grandfather smiled and kissed him on the forehead. "You know, I had planned on us working today, but instead I think we should go fishing," grinned Shakem. "What do you think?" Akeem shook his head yes.

The next day Akeem got up early. He rushed to his grandfather's house, and they made off toward the river. When they arrived, they walked through the mass of tradesmen until they found Jack. Jack was busy trading with a woman who had brought some handmade rugs. He looked through the stack checking each one for quality. Then he rubbed his chin and thought for a minute. Then he nodded his head *yes*. The woman smiled, and began to pick through Jack's assortment of wares to find the things she needed.

Jack saw Shakem and Akeem approaching. His loud booming voice greeted them first. "Well, my friends, welcome, and how are ya today?" he asked as he shook Shakem's hand.

"We are well," smiled Shakem. Akeem grinned and shook Jack's hand just as his grandfather did, then turned and began picking curiously through Jack's pelts.

Jack turned back at Shakem, "And what would you be needin' to trade for today?"

"I broke my hoe a couple of days ago digging in my garden, and I need to get a new handle." He paused for a moment glancing at Akeem then continued, "...and I was thinking, it might be time to get Akeem a knife."

Akeem, who had been looking around, spun in the direction of his grandfather. "Oh, Grandfather, do you mean it?!" he asked as he grabbed Shakem and squeezed him tight. Shakem laughed and nodded *yes*.

Jack turned and motioned them to follow. "I've got just the thing right over here." He led them over to a stockpile of tools. There he picked up a burlap sack and unwrapped it carefully. Inside were several knives. There were knives for working, knives for cooking, knives for hunting, and then... there it was... a large pocketknife with a smooth grey-black handle.

Jack picked it up then opened it. The blade was about five inches long and very sharp. "A knife like this is very dangerous if it's not handled right," he said to Akeem.

Akeem nodded, "Can... can I hold it?"

Jack handed the knife to Akeem, and Akeem ran his fingers over the handle. It was beautiful. Carefully, he ran his fingers over the sharp blade. Then he looked at his grandfather with impatient excitement, "Oh, Grandfather can... can I please have it? I'll be careful."

Shakem nodded *yes*, and Akeem jumped to hug him again, this time with the open knife still in his hand. Shakem and Jack both protested, "Hey, hey, careful with that." Akeem smiled sheepishly and gently closed the knife.

Jack smiled and shook his head as he wrapped the other knives back up in the burlap and put them away. "Now, let's see about that hoe," he said as he led them to the pile of tools.

Akeem followed them with his feet, but his mind and his eyes were on his knife. He was thinking of all the adventures he would have with it. Shakem and Jack were talking in the background, but Akeem didn't hear a word.

Jack was asking Shakem if Akeem could ride down the river with him. Shakem had agreed to it, as long as Akeem would be back before sunset. When Shakem was done trading, he turned and asked, "Akeem, did you hear that? Would you like to go with Jack on the river today?"

Akeem looked at the two men in astonishment, then bear-hugged them both. Akeem's heart was racing. This was his dream come true, to go trading on the river. He could hardly believe it. Shakem and Jack finished their business. An antsy Akeem said goodbye to his grandfather and followed Jack back to his canoe.

The woman with the rugs had picked out the supplies she needed. Jack bargained back and forth with her. She wanted more for her rugs than Jack wanted to trade. Finally, they came to an agreement. As the afternoon went on, Akeem helped get items for people and arranged their goods which they traded into piles.

When lunchtime came, Jack traded some of the other merchants for fresh melons, some cheese and a loaf of bread. Jack had many items in his stock, but he did not carry food or animals. He asked Akeem to cut the melons.

Akeem, seeing an opportunity to use his new knife, was delighted! He cut the melons, then the cheese, then the bread. He hoped Jack wouldn't mind. Then he rinsed his knife off in the water and dried it on his shorts. When they were done with their lunch, the crowd had died down and Jack decided it was time to go upriver.

Akeem helped him pack the canoe. First, they laid the tools in the bottom because they were the longest. They laid the rugs over the tools and put clay pots and baskets on top of the rugs. Then there were animal skins and even a couple of bamboo chairs. When the canoe was loaded, Jack handed Akeem an old cigar box. "Keep your eye on that one, Matey," he said.

Akeem opened the lid and looked inside. It was Jack's money. There were coins and paper bills and even some valuable stones and chains. Akeem put it in the canoe under the bench where he was going to sit. He climbed in the front of the canoe, and Jack got in the back. Jack told Akeem to take the long pole from inside the canoe and stand in the front end to steer. Jack had the oars in the back.

"Akeem, ya' push off with the pole, ya' see, and I'll start rowing backwards." Akeem did as Jack said. The canoe moved only slightly, since it was very heavy when it was all loaded down. That's all right, give it another try there, Mate."

Akeem pushed again, and this time he used all his strength. The canoe started to pull backward out of the muddy edge. Akeem repositioned the pole and pushed again. The canoe started to float. They were free from the bank.

"Now, push to the left!" shouted Jack. Akeem did. This turned the canoe so that it was heading straight upriver. "That's good," said Jack as he started rowing.

The river was wide at the port where Akeem and his grandfather traded, but there were places where the river grew very narrow and shallow. Akeem sat down and laid the pole inside the canoe. Jack paddled first on one side of the canoe then the other. This kept the canoe on a straight course.

They traveled for quite a while and saw a herd of gazelles grazing and drinking from the river's edge. Later, they spotted some rhinoceros off in the distance. Then the river turned and grew narrower. "You'd better get the pole out just in case," said Jack. Akeem did as he was told.

The river seemed to be closing in on them. The further they went, the narrower it became. Along the left side up in front of them was a row of trees where a pack of chimpanzees were living. They chattered and screeched at the canoe. "You'd better make sure to steer clear of them, mate" said Jack. "Those beasts can be extremely dangerous when they feel threatened."

Akeem's excitement began to turn to uneasiness. He stood to his feet and positioned the pole. He had butterflies in his stomach. They floated along and, just as they were in front of the trees, Akeem glanced to the other side. There, entering the water's edge, was an eight-foot crocodile.

Akeem was terrified! He whipped the pole around and stuck it in the mud on the river bottom on the right side of the canoe. He pushed with all his might to turn them away from the crocodile. When he did this, it turned them right into the left bank under the chimpanzees. The monkeys screeched and squalled at them. Several of the large males came down to the lower branches and were just above Akeem's head, batting at him with their long arms and screeching loudly.

The croc on the other side of the river started toward the boat and Jack slapped his paddle on the water several times- hard. The crocodile turned and began to lazily swim down river. Jack looked at Akeem. Akeem was scared senseless. He was frozen in place. A large male chimp was just over him and was screaming furiously and swinging from branch to branch reaching for Akeem.

Jack jumped over his wares to the front of the canoe and grabbed the pole from Akeem's hand. He pushed Akeem down into the bottom of the canoe and shoved the pole hard into the river's edge. He pushed with all his might as the large chimp took a hard swing at the two of them. The canoe floated backward as the chimp lost his grip and fell into the water. The chimp climbed out onto the bank and stood screeching, raising his arms to them and showing his teeth. Jack jumped to the back of the canoe and started rowing them quickly upstream.

Akeem was still in the bottom of the boat. His heart was pounding, and he was breathless from fright. Jack had known just what to do. He had saved them. Akeem sat up on the bench. He felt foolish, and thought the whole ordeal was his fault. If he hadn't panicked when he saw the crocodile, none of it would have happened. From then on, Akeem was quiet and did nothing without being asked to do it.

Akeem was sad as he walked home that evening. His desire to be a great trader had been crushed. He was not brave. He didn't know anything thing about maneuvering up and down the river or about trading for that matter. He had been thinking too highly of himself and had been humbled fast.

Suddenly, he heard a voice from deep inside. "Akeem, My great warrior. You are sad because you feel that you didn't measure up to the world's standards. I tell that I have very different standards. I call you to a new kind of bravery, one that will stand up in the face of adversity and boldly proclaim My word. I have great plans for you. You will go trading on the river. By My hand, I will lead you into this, but riches and fame must not be your goal, for I desire a pure man that will hear My voice and do My deeds. You will meet many people and go many places, and it will be high-adventure of the best kind. Nothing fulfills the heart like the plan I have for you. You will not be disappointed, but will say, 'My God has given me the desire of my heart.' Do not cry for today. For today, you have found humility and this, too, was My plan for you. Be encouraged, brave one!"

As Akeem walked along, he thought of God's words to him. He found great comfort and peace in them. He wanted to tell his grandfather, but it was getting late, and he needed to go straight home so his mother wouldn't worry.

That night at dinner, Akeem and his mother talked about his father. They remembered good times and funny moments. Kamaria looked at Akeem. "Your father would be very proud of you," she said. Akeem was glad she had told him that.

After dinner, Akeem helped his mother with the dishes, and they laughed and splashed each other as they were cleaning up. Then they made a pumpkin pudding for dessert. Sugar was very scarce. They didn't have dessert often, so this was a special treat. They sat together in the front room as Kamaria sat reading. Akeem grew very sleepy. His head nodded and dropped. Kamaria closed her book and nudged him. "There, that's enough, you had better go to bed. You are very tired."

That night Akeem had a dream. He saw himself as a young man, boarding a large ship headed for another country. His bags were packed and being loaded. He was leaving from a very large port in a busy city. He took a place along the rail of the ship and looked for his mother in the crowd. They found each other and waved. He was taking a journey to another country. He didn't know where he was headed in the dream, but he knew it had something to do with his destiny, and he was very excited in his dream.

The next morning, Akeem awoke after his mom had already left for work. As he was getting his breakfast, he felt a gentle nudge in his heart, like someone was trying to get his attention. Akeem ate slowly and prayed as he ate. He didn't want to hurry out.

After he was finished eating, he went and lay on his bed and continued to pray. He saw a picture of himself. He was sitting at Jesus' feet with his head in His lap. Akeem felt such incredible love and acceptance. "Oh, Jesus, thank You for loving me. Thank You for coming and dying for me. There is no one like You."

Akeem sat on his bed for a long time, singing songs that he knew from the mission about how good God is, but it seemed like only a few minutes. He didn't want to stop. "I don't care if I ever go trading. I just want to know You and hear You."

As Akeem prayed, he truly felt everything he was saying. He felt so close to God, like He was his best friend, but even closer than that, like He was his father. He stayed there for a long time not saying anything, just enjoying the warmth he felt as he prayed.

Akeem got to his grandfather's very late that day. "Ah, there you are, my child! I thought you were never going to come today."

Akeem just smiled slightly to acknowledge him. Akeem wanted to tell him why he had been so late, but it felt like it was meant just for him. Instead, he asked what he could do to help.

"Moswen asked me to come and fix their table. We'll need to take my tools." Akeem nodded and went to get them.

When they got there, Moswen was at work and Neema was inside holding baby Keasha. Keasha was sick, and she had been crying all morning. Although she greeted them warmly, it was obvious she was frustrated and tired and was losing her patience with Keasha. Shakem and Akeem started working on the table, but were distracted by Keasha's crying.

Finally, Neema sat down and said "I'm not sure what to do for her." Shakem put down his tool and went over to her. "There, there, Neema. What you are doing is very important. Do not grow weary. These times with little ones can be very trying."

"Neema, we should pray for her." Neema nodded yes. Together, the two of them held the baby and started praying for her. Akeem was standing nearby; he felt he should pray with them, but then thought, "No, I'm just a kid."

Then Akeem heard God's voice say, "If you will pray for Keasha, I will heal her." Akeem was a little nervous. He had never prayed for anyone before, what if he hadn't really heard God? He fidgeted nervously as he tried to decide what to do, but then impulsively hopped up and walked over to put his hand on her. He prayed under his breath, "God, please heal her." When he prayed he could feel something. After a few minutes the baby stilled and then fell to sleep! Her fever had already begun to break. A relieved and happy Neema made them lunch, and they fell into an easy relaxed conversation of the latest events around the village. They finished the table and went home.

# CHAPTER 6

—᙭—

That school year went by quickly. Akeem prayed often. No longer did he utter the simple prayers of a child, but found his heart yearning to talk to God at all times in the day. A wonderful transformation was taking place inside Akeem. He had always loved Him, but now his determination to get to know God had a new intensity.

The fantasies of being a tradesman gave way to a deep desire to follow whatever plan God had for his life. He found himself constantly mentioning his faith in his conversations. His eyes shone with excitement as he retold his grandfather's stories to the neighborhood children, speaking to them of the missionary and how he brought his friend Jesus to their tribe.

It was almost time for school to be out again for the summer. Akeem was twelve and getting very tall. He looked forward to long summer days with his grandfather. During those last few weeks of school Akeem was especially impatient one day to see his grandfather because he had something to show him.

"Grandfather, Grandfather!" shouted Akeem as he ran into Shakem's hut. "Look, I've finished it." Akeem held out a small canoe in the palm of his hand. He had whittled it out of a stick with his knife. He was very proud.

Shakem picked it up and examined it closer. "Well, that's a fine job you've done, Akeem," he said as he patted Akeem on the back. Akeem had grown several inches and was up to his grandfather's chin. "You'll be a fine carver soon. Maybe you'll even be able to make things to trade at the river. That reminds me, I need to get some seed for my garden. We'll need to go down to the river again this afternoon to get some. Why don't you gather up those few baskets over there and we'll trade them." Akeem nodded, and he and Shakem started out for the river.

It was late by the time they got there. The crowd was small, and many of the merchants had already packed up their wares and were paddling downstream. Jack Henry was just beginning to load his canoe when they found him. "Well, good-aye, mates!" He smiled as he shook their hands. "Wasn't intending on seeing the two of you today."

"I need some seed," said Shakem, "to get my vegetables planted."

Jack took a puff off of the end of his cigarette and flicked it into the water. "Got some just the other day," he said as he turned and started digging under some burlap sacks. "Akeem, I was just thinking about you," continued Jack. Akeem was pleased. Jack kept looking for the seed as he talked. "I'm thinkin' it's time for me to move on. Fact of the matter is, I'm missin' the outback. Anyway, I was thinkin', I can't just leave my canoe sittin' on the river bank. So, I was thinkin' about givin' it to you," said Jack as he pulled out the seed and turned around toward them.

Akeem was stunned. "Me?" he stammered, "but, but I don't have any money."

"I didn't say I was gonna sell it to ya. I said I was gonna give it to ya. That is, if it's ok with your grandpa and, of course, your ma."

Akeem's gaze shot to his grandfather. "Oh, Grandfather, can I, can I, please?"

Shakem nodded his head slowly. "I'll talk to your mother. You're about old enough. I think it would be good for you."

Akeem could hardly contain his excitement. "Now, you'll have to watch out for them crocs!" joked Jack as he punched him in the arm. Akeem was a little embarrassed. He had never told his grandfather about the incident with the crocodile. Shakem looked at the two of them a little puzzled.

Akeem moved in closer to the canoe and rubbed his hand along the side. The canoe was not new by any means. The dark green paint was scratched and peeling. There were several dents up and down the sides. Even the wooden planks set inside for seats were cracked and warped, but to Akeem it was perfect. He walked around it inspecting and admiring it. He just couldn't believe it.

Then his thoughts were interrupted. "Akeem, we need to be going now," said his grandfather. Then he added, "Don't worry, son. I'll talk to your mother about the canoe."

After school the next day, Akeem felt anxious. He was ready for summer vacation to begin. There were still three weeks left in the school year. He paced back and forth across the kitchen floor as he ate a slice of bread. He tried to think of something to do.

Frustrated, he went to get his knife and a piece of wood to carve. Then he realized that he had finished whittling the last piece he had. He needed to go outside of town to get some. He was relieved to finally have somewhere to go. He stopped by his grandfather's house on the way out of town to let him know what he was doing.

As he walked along, he kicked a rock in the road. He was thinking about his canoe and all the adventures he would have during the summer. He had walked about a mile from town when, suddenly, he caught sight of something out of the corner of his eye. He lifted his head in that direction. It was a large leopard chasing a white crane. The bird ran on its long legs and tried to fly away, but with one swift pounce the leopard was upon him.

Akeem watched as the leopard ate his dinner. Then suddenly, the leopard stopped eating and looked right in Akeem's direction. Akeem was startled. It was Trakee. "Trakee!" said Akeem out loud, but not loud enough for Trakee to hear him. "You are alright!"

The two stared at each other for another minute. Then the leopard went back to eating his prey. When he had finished, he got up and began to lightly run in the opposite direction. Akeem watched him as he got further and further away and wondered if Trakee had recognized him. He thought he probably had not. Akeem turned and continued walking picking up small pieces of wood as he thought about Trakee. God had protected him. "Thank You," whispered Akeem.

The afternoon was hot, hotter than usual. Akeem found a large tree to sit under. He took out his knife and whittled on a stick. The sweat was beading on his brow, and he wiped it with his arm. Akeem suddenly felt that familiar tugging on his heart. He closed his eyes and laid his hands in his lap. He prayed under his breath.

"Yes, Lord?"

"Akeem, I have such love for you and your mother. She has raised you to know My Word. But there will come a time when you will have to leave her to go on to the next step I have for your life. Will you be one of My workmen?"

Akeem knew he could not answer this question flippantly. Once he had made his decision, there would be no turning back. He searched his heart.

Then after a couple of minutes, he answered, "Yes, God, I will be one of Your workmen. I want my life to count for You. If You will help me, I will devote my life to You."

"Good," he heard God say, "you have pleased Me very much, for I have a very special work for you. I need you to go to another country for me. Once the people of this country loved Me with all their hearts and wanted very much to please Me. But now they seek worldly gain and have lost the love for their neighbor. My heart breaks for this nation for they are very special to Me. I will not turn My back on them. I will never turn My back on them for I love them. Oh, Akeem, I need you to go. I need you to remind them of what their purpose is."

Akeem could see Jesus crying over this nation. His love for them was vast, and He so desperately wanted them to come back to Him. In that moment, Akeem felt the heart of God. He wanted to go to these people and remind them of Jesus and His great call on their country. "Where is it, God? Where do You want me to go?"

"To America, Akeem. I am sending you to America." There was a long pause as Akeem thought of everything he had ever heard about America.

Then his thoughts were interrupted by the voice of God. "There is much work to be done, but I tell you that if you will obey Me and go, I will use you greatly in that country. For My plans for them are for good and not for hurt. I promised it to their forefathers. I will repay goodness to the thousandth generation says the Lord, and My Word will never come back void. Oh, Akeem, you must go, you must go."

Akeem felt God's compassion and love for America and now had His heart for this country.

His thoughts turned toward what he would do to prepare to go...

God was beginning to write a new story in Akeem's life...in America.

# *Journal Pages*

*Akeem*

# MEET THE AUTHOR

—⋙—

T RACEE NEWMAN believes in raising kids to hear God so they can find His direction for their lives. She is the mother of three grown children all of whom are following after God. Tracee shaped her career in the publishing industry through several years at Charisma Media and Xulon Press. She has been involved in church leadership throughout her adult life, concentrating on hospitality and event planning. She is currently pastoring with her husband Don at Crown Pointe Life Center in Orlando, which they planted.

This is the first in a series of three books specifically for children and promises to be an excellent resource for parents who are seeking to raise children to know God.

# ACKNOWLEDGMENTS

—◆—

F irst, I'd like to thank my freelance copy editor and daughter Brittnee Newman. Your insights and hard work brought this project to life again and I so enjoyed our time together working on it.

Ashlee, my other daughter, and Hunter, my son, thank you for painting with me in my room while I told you this story and what I felt God was telling me to do with it. I cherish the memories of all the Mrs. Florida America pageants you went to while I was trying to build a platform to get it published from.

For Xulon Press and all my friends who work there, thank you for making self-publishing possible for authors like me who have a story they feel God has given them to write.

Don Newman, my husband, thank you for being on board with me through all the time this took and for so many other things.

Thank you to my parents Hank and Darlene Leider and all my extended family for believing in me. To Lee and Paislee for making our lives become fuller. I love all of you so much.

To our special friends Jeff and Linda Welker, who have been with Don and I since the beginning, we value your friendship so much. Thank you as well to all the other friends and acquaintances along the way that have helped and supported me.

Finally, to my future readers, I pray you enjoy reading these books and that they become a favorite part of your childhood memories.

CPSIA information can be obtained at www.ICGtesting.com
Printed in the USA
LVOW061848040712

288779LV00001B/6/P